BRAVE

Monsters Love School

Copyright © 2014 by Mike Austin • All rights reserved. Manufactured in China. • No part of this book may be used or reproduced in any manner whatsoever without written permission except in the case of brief quotations embodied in critical articles and reviews. For information address HarperCollins Children's Books, a division of HarperCollins Publishers, 10 East 53rd Street, New York, NY 10022. • www.harpercollinschildrens.com • Library of Congress Cataloging-in-Publication Data Austin, Mike, date, author, illustrator. Monsters love school / written and illustrated by Mike Austin. — First Edition. • pages cm • Summary: Nervous monsters attending school for the first time learn new things, make friends, and

sample Chef Ods's special School Gruel. ISBN 978-0-06-228618-5 (hardcover bdg.) [1. First day of school—Fiction. 2. Schools—Fiction. 3. Monsters—Fiction.] I. Title. PZ7.A9253Mos 2014 [E]—dc23 2013032822 CIP AC • The artist used his favorite monster pencils, monster crayons, monster ink and brushes, a scanner, and Adobe Photoshop to create the digital illustrations for this book. • Typography by Mike Austin 14 15 16 17 18 SCP 10 9 8 7 6 5 4 3 2 1 ❖ First Edition

For Tien and Reid

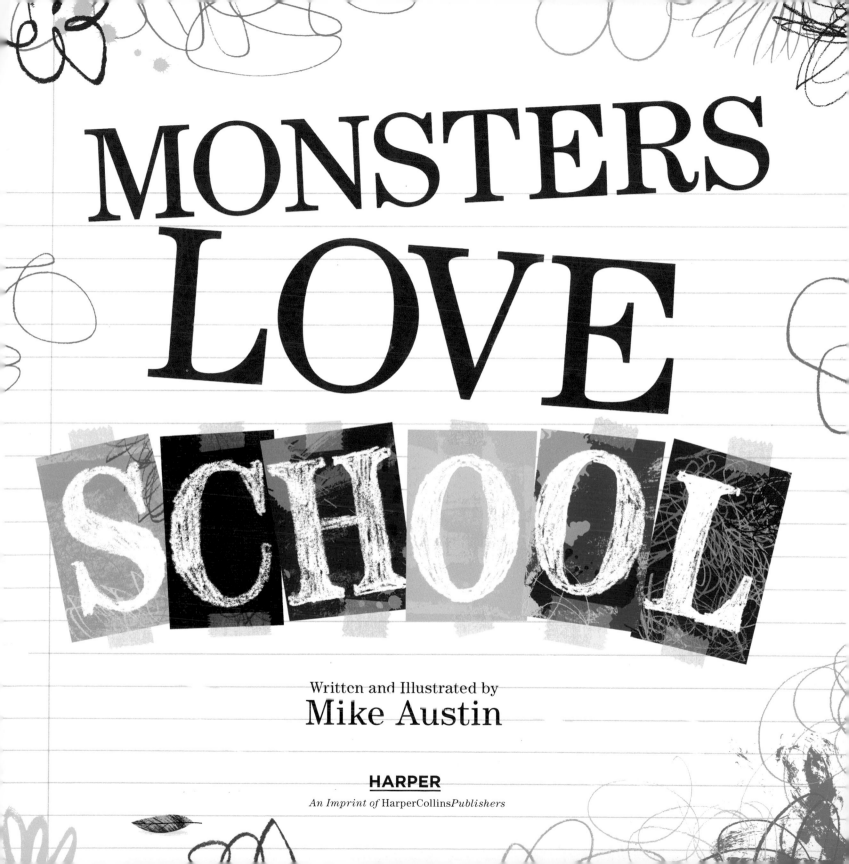

MONSTERS LOVE SCHOOL

Written and Illustrated by
Mike Austin

HARPER

An Imprint of HarperCollinsPublishers

Brave little monsters love big adventures!

Diving and swinging, splashing and singing all summer long.

"Row, row, row your monster, gently through the swamp!"

But summer has come to an end.

Now it's time to get ready for the biggest adventure of all . . .

"We need a backpack filled with special supplies for this big adventure! Check the list!" says Greeny.

School Supply Checklist

- ☐ Tape
- ☐ Paper
- ☐ Stapler
- ☐ Ruler
- ☐ Crayons
- ☐ Glue
- ☐ Folders
- ☐ Pencils
- ☐ Eraser
- ☐ Paint
- ☐ Scissors
- ☐ Lunc

"Tape, CHECK!
Paper, CHECK!
Ruler, CHECK!"

"Lunch box,
CHECK!
Crayons,
CHECK!"

"What if I get
hungry? When
do we eat?"
asks Blue.

"We eat at
lunchtime
in the cafeteria,"
says Little Gray.

"LET'S GO,
BUDDY!"

"Good morning!" says Miss Wiggles.

"What if no one likes me?" worries Blue.

"You're going to make lots of new friends!" says Little Gray.

"Wiggle, wiggle!"

Miss Wiggles sings:

"Wiggle, wiggle, cross the street.
Off to school, now move those feet!"

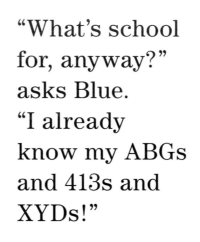

"What's school
for, anyway?"
asks Blue.
"I already
know my ABGs
and 413s and
XYDs!"

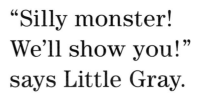

"Silly monster!
We'll show you!"
says Little Gray.

Principal Blinkin says, "School is for learning your
ABCs
and 123s
and XYZs!"

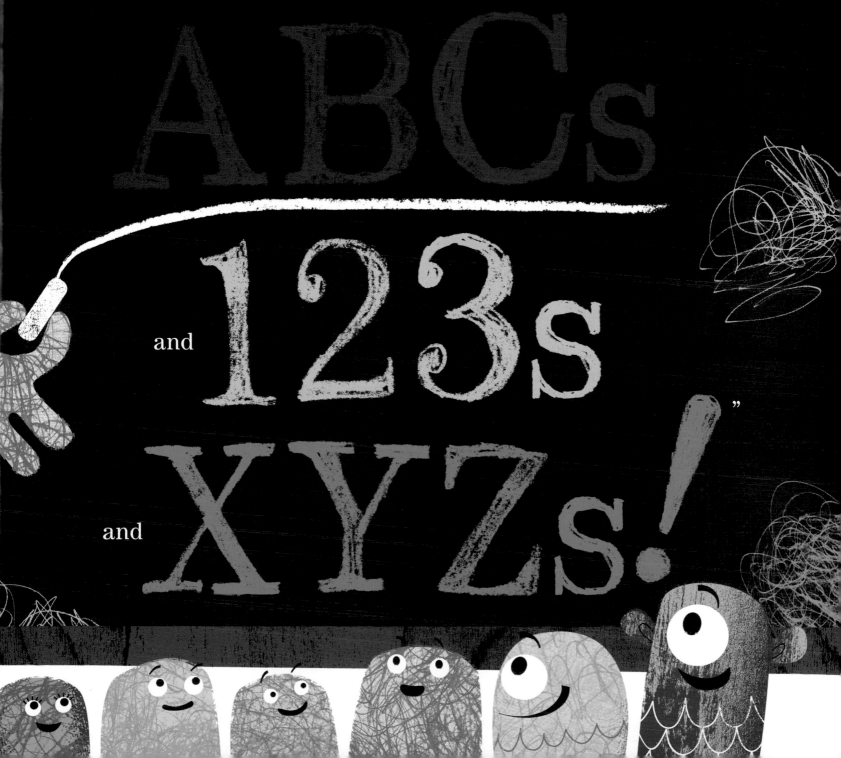

"School is for painting and folding and pasting!"
says Miss Scribble, the art teacher.

"I made a
superhero mask!
GRRRRR!"
says Blue.

"I made a
mustache!"
says Little Gray.

"I made a
fancy hat fit
for a queen!
I LOVE
art class!"
says Pinky.

GREEN

RED

GLUE

BROWN

"I made a mistake! PLEASE HELP!" says Goo.

"That's okay— everybody makes mistakes. I'll help you fix it!" says Miss Scribble.

BLUE

GLUE

GLUE

YELLOW

WHITE

"School is for making new friends!" says Pinky.

"I love your fancy hat!
Nice job, your majesty!"

"I LOVE RECESS!"

"Why, thank you!
Your superhero mask
is quite splendid!"

"School is for reading and writing and spelling!" says Miss Spel.

"Can you spell *monster*?"

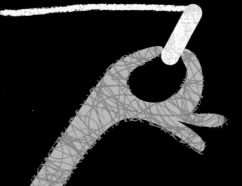

"M-O-N-ST-E-R!"

"M-O-N-ST-E-R!"

"M-U-N-Z-D-E-R?"

~~Munster~~
Monster

"H-U-N-G-R-Y!
When do we eat?!"

"M-O-N-S-T-E-R!"

"School is for trying new things!" says Chef Octi.
"Like my delicious, nutritious, world-famous

SCHOOL GRUEL!"

"Yummy, yummy!
Monsters drool
for school gruel!"

Mrs. Hiss says, "School is for learning your monster hisssssssssssssssstory!"

ABRAHAM MONSTER LINCOLN

MONSTER HISTORY

"Mrs. Hiss's hissstory classs is AWESSSSSOME!"

"Now it's time for Explorer Book Club!" says Mr. Reed, the librarian.

"And let's hear it for Singing Club!" shouts Miss Warble.
"Give it up for our newest group—
the HI
NOTES!"

"So beautiful!"
sniffles Pinky.

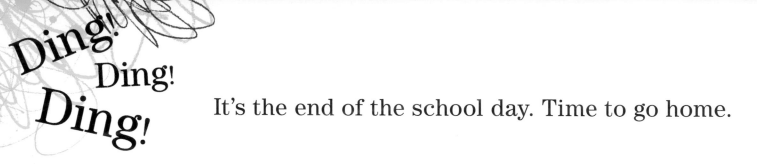

Ding! Ding! Ding!

It's the end of the school day. Time to go home.

"Hi, Blue!"
says Little Gray.
"How was your
first day of school?"

"I was kind of scared, but now I'm not.
I'm learning my ABCs and 123s and XYZs.
I made a cool new superhero mask in art class.
I met lots of new friends.
I'm learning to read and write and spell.
I ate school gruel and tomorrow I'm bringing lunch.
I'm learning my monster history.
Book club at the library is AWESOME!
I sang funny songs.
I had fun!

And you know
what else?